Homework Hassles

by ABBY KLEIN

illustrated by
JOHN MCKINLEY

SCHOLASTIC INC.
New York Toronto London Auckland Sydney
Mexico City New Delhi Hong Kong Buenos Aires

To Mom and Dad—
thanks for always
being there for me.
I love you.
—A. K.

THE BLUE SKY PRESS

Text copyright © 2004 by Abby Klein
Illustrations copyright © 2004 by John McKinley
All rights reserved.

Special thanks to Robert Martin Staenberg.

No part of this publication may be reproduced, stored in
a retrieval system, or transmitted in any form or by any means,
electronic, mechanical, photocopying, recording, or otherwise,
without written permission of the publisher. For information
regarding permission, please write to: Permissions Department,
Scholastic Inc., 557 Broadway, New York, New York 10012.
SCHOLASTIC, THE BLUE SKY PRESS, and associated logos are
trademarks and/or registered trademarks of Scholastic Inc.
ISBN-13: 978-0-439-55600-2 / ISBN-10: 0-439-55600-7
22 21 20 19 18 17 16   10 11 12 13
Printed in the United States of America 40
First Scholastic paperback printing, November 2004

CHAPTERS

I have a problem.

A really, really, big problem.

I hate doing homework, and
I have a report due next week.

Let me tell you about it.

CHAPTER 1

The Assignment

"OK, class," said our teacher, Mrs. Wushy. "Please listen carefully. I'm going to tell you about a very special homework assignment."

The class groaned.

"I think you will all really enjoy this assignment," Mrs. Wushy continued. "Since we have been studying nocturnal animals, I thought it would be fun if you each chose a nocturnal animal to learn a little more about and then shared what you've learned with the class."

"Oh, I want to do a bunny," said Chloe, wrinkling up her nose. "They're so soft, and cuddly, and cute."

"Bunnies?" Max snickered. "You can't do a bunny, stupid, because bunnies are not nocturnal."

"Max, how many times have I told you not to use the word 'stupid'?" Mrs. Wushy asked.

"Sorry," he mumbled.

"But you are correct," said Mrs. Wushy. "Bunnies are not nocturnal animals. Who remembers what nocturnal means?"

Robbie's hand shot up. Robbie is my best friend, and he is really smart. He is like a walking encyclopedia of science.

"Yes, Robbie. Can you please tell us what nocturnal means?"

"If something is nocturnal, then it is awake at night and sleeps during the day. Humans are not nocturnal. We are diurnal. We like to sleep at night and are awake during the day."

"Very good, Robbie. That's right. Nocturnal animals do all of their work at night. They eat, hunt, and play when it is dark."

"Oooh, that's scary," said Chloe. "I'm glad I'm not nocturnal. I'm scared of the dark," she said, pretending to shiver.

Just then, Max, who was sitting right behind her, leaned over and shouted, "BOO!" in her ear.

Chloe jumped and screamed like a baby, "AHHHHHHHH!"

Max was rolling around on the floor, laughing hysterically.

Chloe stood up, pouting, hands on her hips, and whined, "Did you see what he did, Mrs. Wushy? I think he should get a time-out!"

"Chloe," said Mrs. Wushy, "you are not the teacher. I will take care of this. Max, you need to apologize to Chloe."

"Sorry I scared you, little baby," he said, still laughing.

"All right, that's enough, Max. Please go sit in that chair over there."

Max got up to go sit in the chair on the other side of the room, and Chloe

smoothed her ruffled, pink, party dress and sat back down on the rug. I don't know why she wears party dresses to school. She's such a little fancy-pants!

"OK, now where were we?" Mrs. Wushy said and sighed. "Oh yes. Does anyone know what animal they'd like to do?"

Robbie raised his hand. "I want to do geckos because I have a leopard gecko named Violet at home. I could stay up late and study her."

"Yes, Jessie," said Mrs. Wushy.

"I'll do raccoons. My *abuela* calls them *bandidos* because they look just like little robbers with their black masks."

"Hey, that's what I wanted to do!" Max called out from his chair.

"Well," said Mrs. Wushy, "maybe next time you'll be a better listener, and you can pick first. But for this assignment, Jessie gets to do raccoons."

"Awww. That's not fair, Mrs. Wushy," Max complained.

"Max, not another word from you."

Other kids kept raising their hands. It seemed as if everyone in the class had an idea except me.

"Freddy," said Mrs. Wushy, "do you have any ideas?"

"Nope."

"Well, you have time to think about it. Everyone will give a little report to the class next week. You might also want to include some pictures of your animals. I wrote the assignment down on this paper, so make sure you show it to your parents."

"This is going to be so cool," Robbie whispered excitedly.

"Yeah, right," I whispered back. "Maybe for you, Brainiac. Hey, do you want to bring Violet over tonight, and we can stay up late and watch what she does at night?"

"Are you kidding? Your mother would never let me bring a lizard into your house."

"Yeah, that's true. Well, you and I can stay up late anyway, and see what it's like to be nocturnal."

"Yeah. Maybe we'll even stay up all night," Robbie said.

"Now you're talking. I've never stayed up all night before. Great idea! I can't wait!"

CHAPTER 2

Hanging Around

I could hardly wait for Robbie to come over. We had big plans for the night.

I strolled into the kitchen where my mom was baking brownies for a special chocolate-fudge-brownie sundae dessert. It was Robbie's and my favorite: a thick, rich chocolate brownie, two scoops of vanilla ice cream, lots of fudge sauce, rainbow sprinkles, whipped cream, and a cherry on top. "Mmmm, those smell yummy!" I said.

"Mom, how much longer until Robbie gets here?"

"Boy, you've sure got ants in your pants," my mom said. "Do you two have something special planned for tonight?"

"No, just the usual," I answered. There was no way I was going to let her in on our little secret. She would never let us stay up all night. Never.

"Like what do you have planned?"

"Oh, I don't know. Watch some TV, play Trouble, trade baseball cards, tell each other ghost stories."

"Trouble?" she asked. "What kind of trouble are you planning on getting into?"

"No, Mom, the game, Trouble. You know, the one where you pop that little bubble to roll the dice."

"Oh, good. For a minute there you had

me worried that you two were planning on getting into trouble."

Just then my big sister, Suzie, walked into the room. "Trouble? Who's getting into trouble?" she asked. "What did Freddy do this time, Mom?"

"Just shut up, Booger Breath!" I said. "I didn't do anything."

"That's what you always say," she answered, sticking her tongue out.

"Leave me alone, Brat. Mom and I were

just talking about tonight, and it's none of your beeswax."

"Ugh," Suzie groaned. "I forgot you have your little sleepover tonight. I'll have double trouble."

"All right, Suzie, that's enough," my mom said. "Stop picking on Freddy."

"Well, you guys better leave me alone this time," Suzie continued. "Or you'll be sorry," she whispered in my ear.

"What are you talking about, Suzie?" my mom asked.

"Don't you remember, Mom? The last time Robbie slept over, they put a snail in my bed, and when I got in, it started to crawl up my leg. It was the grossest thing that's ever happened to me. I didn't want to get in my bed for a week!"

"We didn't put it there," I said, giggling. "It crawled there all by itself. We left it on the bathroom mirror to see what kind of cool design the snail trail would make, but when we came back to check on it, it was gone. I can't help it that it decided to crawl into your bed."

"*You* brought that snail into the house?" my mom said. "How many times have I told you not to bring animals into this house? Especially slimy ones!"

My mom is a Neat Freak. We aren't allowed to eat anywhere except in the kitchen, and the only pet I'm allowed to have is my goldfish, Mako, because he doesn't shed, smell, or have a cage that needs cleaning.

"Sorry, Mom. I promise it won't happen again," I said.

"Yeah, right," Suzie snickered.

Just when I thought I couldn't wait any longer, the doorbell rang. "That must be Robbie. I'll get it!" I called, as I ran to the door.

The night was just beginning.

CHAPTER 3

The Plan

I loved when Robbie came to sleep over. We always had so much fun. He was really good at making up secret plans, and tonight's plan was the best one ever.

My parents had already tucked us in. They thought the two of us were asleep. I turned on my special sharkhead flashlight. "How are we going to stay up all night?" I whispered. "Last year on Christmas Eve, I tried to stay up all night and wait for Santa, but I fell asleep before he came." I hit my forehead with the palm of my hand. "Think, think, think."

"Easy," said Robbie. "We'll read scary stories from your new shark book, *Monsters of the Deep*, play Space Invaders with our Commander Upchuck figures, eat lots of candy . . ."

"Candy?" I asked. "I don't have any candy. You know my mom doesn't let me eat anything in my room."

"I know," Robbie said, smiling. "That's why I hid some in my backpack: jelly beans, chocolate bars, lollipops—the kind that take forever to suck."

"You're awesome!" I said, hugging him. "We just have to be extra careful that we don't leave any wrappers lying around."

"And then," Robbie said, "when the house is quiet, and we know for sure that your parents are asleep, we'll sneak out into the backyard and see what kind of nocturnal animals we can find!"

"You mean go outside in the dark?" I asked nervously.

"Yeah. My mom got me these really cool night-vision goggles, and I've been dying to try them out."

"We'll freeze out there."

"Where's your sense of adventure? Why are you being such a fraidy cat?"

"I'm not a fraidy cat."

"Well, you're sure acting like one," Robbie said.

"I just want to make sure that we have it all planned out," I said, "because I don't want to wake up my parents. If they find out that I went outside in the middle of the night, I'll be grounded for life! I did it once before to save that baby bird, Winger, and my dad thought I was some robber. He almost called the police! That night I promised him I would never go outside in the middle of the night again!"

"Stop worrying. They won't find out. I know we have the perfect plan," Robbie reassured me. "We wait until everyone is asleep, and then we go. It'll be great. We can pretend that we're secret agents on a special mission."

Robbie read me scary shark stories by flashlight, and we stuffed ourselves with candy until the light in the hallway went off. That was our signal that everyone had gone to sleep. We waited a little while longer just to be safe. Then I carefully opened my bedroom door and peeked out. "The coast is clear," I whispered to Robbie.

We quietly put our coats on over our pajamas and grabbed our shoes. "You have to carry your shoes and put them on downstairs," I said. "I'm hoping my mom won't hear us if we walk in our socks. Also, put your flashlight in your pocket and keep

it off until we get outside. The night-light is on, so we can see our way down the stairs. Remember to skip the fourth stair from the top. It squeaks."

Robbie gave me a thumbs-up.

This nocturnal adventure was going to be so cool. I waved my hand toward Robbie in a quick "let's go" motion and whispered, "Come on."

CHAPTER 4

In the Dark
of Night

We started to tiptoe down the stairs in our socks. Robbie almost stepped on the fourth step, but I grabbed him just in time and yanked him back.

"Hey, what are you doing?" he asked.

I put my finger to my lips. "Shhhh. That was a close one. Remember, you have to skip that step."

"Oh, yeah," Robbie mouthed, nodding his head.

We made our way down the rest of the stairs and into the kitchen. By the back door, we sat down on the floor to put on our shoes. "What do you want to do when we get out there?" I asked Robbie.

"Let's go exploring, and see what kind of night creatures we can find. With these night-vision goggles, I can see as well as an owl in the dark."

"We still have to whisper when we're outside," I said. "I swear my mom can hear anything."

I tried to turn the latch on the back door. "Rats!" I whispered.

"What?"

"This latch always gets stuck."

"Let me try," Robbie said, pushing me

out of the way. He spit into his hands and then rubbed the spit on the latch.

"Ewww. Gross. What are you doing?"

"I'm trying to lubricate the latch."

"What? Uh, could you speak English, Einstein?"

"I'm trying to get the latch wet. So it slides more easily."

"Well then, why didn't you just say that?" I said.

Robbie rubbed on a little more spit. "Got it!" he said.

The latch turned, and we were finally in the backyard. "Brrrr. It's freezing out here," I said. My teeth were chattering. "How do these nocturnal animals stay warm?"

"They have fur, and they move around

a lot," Robbie said. "Just don't stand still, and you won't be so cold."

We walked to the back of the yard and searched the ground for animal tracks.

"Hey, Freddy, look at this," Robbie said, motioning for me to come closer. "It looks like the footprints of a possum."

"How do you know what possum footprints look like?" I asked.

"I saw them in a book once. I bet it's around here someplace. I'm going to go over there," he said, pointing at my garage, "and see if it's up on the roof."

While Robbie was tracking the possum, I was getting bored, and my fingers were starting to freeze. I decided to keep warm by climbing the tallest tree in my yard.

"I know," I called to Robbie. "You stay on the ground and use your goggles. I'll climb the tree and let you know if I see it from up there."

"You're going to go climb that tree in the dark?"

"Yeah, why not? I've done it so many times I could do it with my eyes closed."

"All right."

As I started to climb up the trunk, I lost my grip and fell to the ground.

"Are you OK?" Robbie whispered.

"Yeah, fine," I answered. "It's hard to get a good grip because my hands are cold.

Now I know why raccoons and possums have sharp claws."

I started back up the tree again, and this time I reached my favorite branch and sat down. I was finally big enough to climb as high as the third branch. "See anything yet?" I called down to Robbie in a whisper.

"No!"

"Me neither."

As I sat in the tree waiting for Robbie to find something, I slowly scooted my body farther out on the branch. Then I gripped the branch with the back of my knees and let go with my hands. "Hey, look at me!" I called to Robbie. "I'm hanging upside down just like a poss . . ."

The next thing I knew, the branch broke, and I hit the ground with a *THUD*!

"AAAAHHHHHHHH!"

CHAPTER 5

Is It Broken?

The emergency room was full of people, even in the middle of the night! We had already been waiting there an hour, and my right arm was killing me. My mom was convinced that it was broken.

"When is it going to be our turn?" Suzie whined. My parents had to wake her up in the middle of the night to come to the hospital with us.

"Don't even start, Suzie," my dad said.

"If anyone should be complaining, it's

Freddy," my mom said, turning to me. "Are you OK, baby?" She had tied a blanket under my arm and around my neck like a sling to keep my arm from moving.

"It really hurts, Mom," I said, sniffling.

"Can you wiggle your fingers like this?" my dad asked, moving all his fingers up and down.

"Nope," I said, wincing in pain.

"Boy, his fingers are so swollen, they look like little sausages," Suzie said.

"If they weren't so swollen, I'd give you a big knuckle sandwich right now," I said, glaring at her.

"Stop it right now, you two," my dad said, gritting his teeth.

Just then, the nurse called my name: "Freddy Thresher."

"Finally," I said and sighed.

"Just follow me, please," she said.

We followed her into an examining room, where she took my blood pressure and carefully unwrapped my arm to get a better look.

"Dr. Carton will be here in a minute," she said as she left the room.

A few minutes later, Dr. Carton came in. "Well, hello there, cutie," she said. "Let's take a look at that arm. Now, tell me—how did this happen?"

"I fell out of a tree," I answered.

"What were you doing in a tree in the middle of the night?"

"Don't ask," my mom answered, rolling her eyes.

"Well, it certainly looks broken to me, but we're going to take an X-ray to be sure.

Freddy and I will be back in a few minutes," she said, smiling.

She put me in a wheelchair and wheeled me down to the X-ray room. She lifted me onto a bed and told me to stay real still. Then she left the room, and I was alone in the dark.

My stomach started to do flip-flops. I

didn't know what was going to happen. I'd never had an X-ray before.

"All done," she said when she came back into the room a minute later.

"That's it?" I asked.

"Yep, that's it."

"Is it broken?" I asked nervously.

"It sure is. A nice, clean break. Let's go tell your parents."

Do we have to? I thought. When this was all over, I was going to get the biggest punishment of my life.

She wheeled me back to the room where Suzie and my parents were all anxiously waiting to hear the news.

"Is it broken, Doctor?" my dad asked.

"I'm afraid so."

"I knew it," my mom said.

"We'll have to put it in a cast."

I suddenly felt sick.

"A cast?" Suzie said. "You are so lucky, Freddy. Casts are so cool. All your friends can sign it, and you don't have to do homework for a whole month!"

Hey, maybe breaking my arm wouldn't be so bad. I kind of liked that part about not having to do homework.

"Oh, Suzie, don't be ridiculous," my mom said. "Breaking your arm is not so lucky."

"Freddy, what color would you like your cast to be?" Dr. Carton asked.

"I thought casts were white," my dad said.

"Not anymore," Dr. Carton said. "Now they come in designer colors."

"Can I have blue-gray?"

"Blue-gray? Why blue-gray?" Dr. Carton asked, puzzled.

"Because that's my favorite color. It's the color of thresher sharks."

"You'll have to excuse him," my dad said. "He's a shark freak."

"Oh," Dr. Carton said, smiling. "Well, I don't have blue-gray, but I have a nice light blue color. How does that sound?"

"Great!" I said.

By the time Dr. Carton got done setting my cast, it was almost 4:00 A.M.

I had stayed up all night after all.

CHAPTER 6

Not So Bad
After All

There were only two bad things about breaking my arm. One, my punishment: I couldn't have a sleepover with Robbie for a whole month. Two, I had to wrap my cast in a plastic bag whenever I took a bath. Because I couldn't get my cast wet, my mom didn't let me play with my sharks in the tub. Otherwise, breaking my arm had its advantages. My parents and my sister had to do a lot of stuff for me.

On Monday morning, my mom had to help me get dressed for school because it was hard for me to lift my arm over my head to put on my shark t-shirt.

"Be careful, baby," my mom said. "Lift your arm slowly. Are you OK?"

"Yeah. But it's still pretty sore, so I don't think I can make my bed."

"Oh, don't be silly, sweetheart. I don't expect you to make your bed. Not with a broken arm. Dr. Carton told you to move it as little as possible."

Not make my bed! This was great! My mom was such a Neat Freak that I usually had to make my bed before I came down for breakfast. And she would do a bed check while I was eating to make sure I had really done it.

"Where's your backpack, honey?" my mom asked. "I'm going to carry it down-stairs for you."

"I think I threw it in the closet."

"Freddy, you know I like you to hang it up on the hook, so it stays nice."

Stays nice? Who was she kidding? No boy's backpack stays nice. If it looks too clean, kids think you're a geek. In fact, when she bought it, I stepped on it with my dirty shoes and dropped it in a mud puddle, just so it wouldn't look brand-new.

She found my backpack, and we went downstairs.

"How's it feel this morning, Sport?" my dad asked, looking up from his paper.

"OK, I guess. But I think it would feel a lot better if I stayed home from school and rested."

"Maybe that's not such a bad idea," my mom said, caressing my head. "This is a rather serious injury. What do you think, Daniel? Should he stay home?"

"What?!" Suzie said, choking on her

cereal. "You're going to let him stay home from school?! That's not fair."

"Suzie, this is none of your business," my dad said.

"But," Suzie whined, "you said we only stay home if we have a temperature, or if we're throwing up, and Freddy isn't hot, and he's not tossing his cookies!"

"Hey, Brat," I said, wagging a finger from my left hand in her face. "You're not my mother."

"Enough!" my dad barked. Then he turned to me. "Freddy, that was a good try, but you're going to school. Dr. Carton said you did not have to miss any school.

You're just not allowed to run around at recess or climb the monkey bars."

Correction—there were three bad things about breaking my arm. "But recess is my favorite part of the day! What am I supposed to do while my friends play Sharks and Minnows? Sit on the bench?"

"Maybe you could play in the playhouse with the girls," Suzie said, smiling.

I stuck my tongue out at her.

"What's wrong with that?" my mom asked. "I think that's a great idea."

"I'll tell you what's wrong with that. I don't want everyone to laugh at me."

"They won't laugh," my mom said.

"Yes, they will. Especially Max—you know, the biggest bully in the whole first grade. He'll laugh and laugh."

"Well, I think you're being silly, but suit

yourself. Hurry up and eat your cereal. I don't want you to be late."

I picked up my spoon and dipped it in the bowl. I started to lift the spoon to my mouth, but my hand was shaking, and I hit my chin instead. Milk and cereal dribbled down my chin and plopped into my lap. "Oh great!" I cried.

"Ha, ha, ha. That was hilarious!" Suzie squealed. "The milk stain makes it look like you peed in your pants!"

"Thanks a lot."

"Suzie," my dad said, "you could be a little nicer to your brother. He's a righty, so he has to get used to doing things with his left hand. It's not as easy as it looks."

"Yeah. I'd like to see *you* eat with your left hand," I said.

"I would, but the bus will be here any

minute," Suzie said, getting up from the table. "I don't want to be late."

"Oh no!" my mom said. "I didn't realize how late it was. Forget the cereal, Freddy. You can take a banana on the bus."

"You'd better hurry up!" Suzie called from the front hall. "I'm not going to wait for you."

"Oh yes you are!" my dad hollered back. "Suzie Marie Thresher, get back in here right now!"

"What?" Suzie said, sticking her head through the kitchen doorway.

"Not only are you going to wait for your brother, but you're going to carry his backpack as well."

"What? You mean that ugly thing with the big fin on the back?"

"Yep."

"You can't be serious. You're joking, right? What am I? His slave?"

"As a matter of fact, for the next few days, you are," my dad said. "He needs all the help he can get."

"Boy, you can say that again," Suzie mumbled as she grabbed my backpack and headed for the door.

CHAPTER 7

King of
the World

"Thanks, Suzie," I said as she dropped my backpack at my classroom door and took off across the yard.

"You're not welcome!" she called over her shoulder.

As soon as I walked into class, all the kids ran up to me and started asking me tons of questions.

Jessie was the first. "Oh my gosh, Freddy! What happened?!"

"Is it broken?" Chloe asked.

"Duh," said Max. "Of course it's broken. Why do you think he has on a cast?"

"Well, you don't have to be so mean," Chloe said, sticking out her tongue. "I was just asking."

Max turned back to me. "So, what

happened? Did you fall off your bike with training wheels?" he snickered.

"No, for your information, I fell out of a tree. A very high tree."

"Oh yeah. How high?" Max asked.

"Oh, I bet I was at least twenty feet off the ground." I glanced over in Robbie's direction and gave him a *please just back me up* kind of look.

"Oh yeah, at *least* twenty feet," Robbie chimed in.

"Yep. I was doing some fancy tricks on a branch, and the branch broke."

"Yeah, he was hanging upside down by his knees," said Robbie.

"No way!" Max said in disbelief. "I didn't think you even knew how to climb a tree."

"Oh yeah, I do it all the time," I said, trying to sound tough.

Jessie gently touched my cast. "Does it hurt a lot, Freddy?"

"It did at first, but not much anymore."

"*Caramba!* You're so brave."

"Well, Freddy," said Mrs. Wushy, "that must have been scary. I'm glad you're OK. I see you broke your right hand, so you'll have to be a lefty for a few weeks. You just let me know if you need any extra help with your work. It might be tough to cut with your left hand."

"Thanks," I said, smiling.

"Can we sign your cast?" Jessie asked.

"Sure."

"That's a great idea, Jessie," Mrs. Wushy

said. "I bet that would make Freddy feel a lot better. I'll go get some permanent markers."

Mrs. Wushy went to get the markers, and I sat down at a table to rest my arm. Robbie came to sit next to me.

"Thanks for playing along back there," I whispered.

"What are friends for?" he whispered back and smiled.

"You know, you're the best friend a guy could have."

"So you're not mad at me for all that happened?" Robbie asked.

"Naw. It's not your fault. I was the one who climbed the tree."

Just then Mrs. Wushy came back. "OK, everyone, let's line up, and you can take turns signing Freddy's cast."

Max, of course, pushed and shoved his way to the front of the line and then wrote his name on it really HUGE. Too bad the markers were permanent.

"The rest of you need to write a little smaller," said Mrs. Wushy, "so that everyone's name will fit."

Chloe bragged, "I know how to write my name in cursive," and then she wrote her name all swirly and fancy. I guess I was supposed to be impressed, but I wasn't.

Jessie signed her name and then drew a little red heart next to it. My stomach did a flip-flop.

When it was Robbie's turn, he wrote, "Best friends forever, Robbie."

After all the kids were finished, Mrs. Wushy drew a big happy face and wrote, "Feel better soon! Love, Mrs. Wushy."

I looked at my cast and smiled. "Thanks, everybody. This looks really, really cool."

It was so great being the center of attention. I felt like I was king of the world.

Then Mrs. Wushy brought me back down to earth.

As everyone went to sit on the rug, she said, "Now remember, boys and girls,

your nocturnal animal reports are due tomorrow. I hope everyone worked hard on them over the weekend."

Oh no! The report. I had forgotten all about it. I still hadn't picked an animal. But why was I worrying? Mrs. Wushy wouldn't make me do it with a broken arm. I raised my hand.

"Yes, Freddy."

"Mrs. Wushy, you don't expect me to do the report with a broken arm, do you?"

"You're lucky, Freddy, because this is not a written report. It's an oral report, so you can still do it. It doesn't involve any writing. All you have to do is talk, so I know you'll do just fine."

The king of the world just became king of the mud!

CHAPTER 8

The Report

That afternoon after school, I begged my mom to let me go over to Robbie's house to do some research for my report. He has his own computer in his room, and he's like a whiz with that thing. He's better than my dad! He said he could help me find information about my animal on the Internet.

"Hey, guys," Robbie's mom said as she came into his room. "I didn't even hear you come in. Sorry about what happened, Freddy. How's your arm feeling?"

"It's OK, Mrs. Jackson."

"I still don't know what the two of you were doing in the backyard in the middle of the night. But I do know one thing for sure. It won't ever happen again! Right, Robbie?"

"Right, Mom."

Robbie's mom stood in the doorway, shaking her head. "Hanging upside down in a tree in the middle of the night. What do you think you are, Freddy? A little bat?"

A bat! That's it! I ran over to Robbie's mom and gave her a big hug. "Thanks, Mrs. Jackson."

"For what?"

"You just gave me a great idea!"

"I did?"

"Yeah. I didn't know which nocturnal animal to pick for my report. But now I know. A bat!"

"Great idea. Let me know if you boys need any help."

"OK. Thanks, Mom," Robbie said as his

mom turned and left. "All right, Freddy. Let's see what we can find."

His fingers started flying over the keys. "Oh, here's a great site for bats. It tells you all kinds of interesting information." He started reading some of it to me. Even

though he's in first grade, he reads better than a fourth grader!

"Most bats eat either fruit or insects."

"Fruit sounds good, but once I ate a cricket, and it made me vomit," I said.

"Thank you for sharing," Robbie said, making a face.

"Anytime," I answered, smiling.

"The largest bat is the flying fox."

"Holy cow!" I said. "Look at that thing. It's huge! I sure hope they don't live around here."

"Don't worry. It says here that they live in Asia."

"That's good, because just looking at that thing could give you nightmares. Yuck!" I said, sticking out my tongue.

"Oh, here's something really cool," Robbie continued. "You can put this in

your report. Bats have sort of a sixth sense, called echolocation, that they use to help them move around in the dark."

"Echolo-what?"

"Echolocation. Insect-eating bats send out high-pitched sound, and then the sound bounces off objects around them

77

and comes back to their ears. This is how they sense if there is a tree they are about to fly into, or if there is an insect near them to eat."

"Hey, I wish I had that sense when I get up to go to the bathroom in the middle of the night. I'm always smacking my face right into the bathroom door!"

"Oh, so that explains why your face looks like that."

"Very funny," I said. "What does it say about hanging upside down?"

"Let's see. It says that bats hang upside down when they are resting, and they wrap their wings around themselves like blankets to keep warm. When a mother bat gives birth, she hangs by her thumb claws with her head up and makes a basket with her body. The baby slides down into it."

"But if there's no nest, then doesn't the egg just fall to the ground and crack when it comes out of the mom?" I asked.

"Bats don't lay eggs."

"They don't?"

"No. Even though they fly, they are not birds. They are mammals."

"What's a mammal?"

"You're a mammal."

"And you're crazy."

"No, really, Freddy. A mammal means that you are born alive, not from an egg, your body has hair, and you drink your mother's milk."

"Oh, I get it. Geez. You sure know about a lot of stuff, Robbie."

"Bat babies are born alive from their moms, and the mom catches them with her body when they come out, so they don't fall to the ground."

"Wow. Bats are pretty interesting. I'm glad I picked them. Can you print that stuff out for me, Robbie?"

"Sure. Just promise me one thing."

"What?"

"You don't go on any night flights tonight."

CHAPTER 9

Help!

After I got home from Robbie's, my mom was helping me organize my report when Suzie walked in.

"What are you doing?"

"I'm trying to practice my report. I have to do it tomorrow."

"What's your stupid report about?" Suzie asked.

"Bats."

"Eww. Gross. Bats suck your blood."

"That's what I used to think, but they're actually really gentle animals. Only the vampire bat drinks blood, and it rarely bites humans. It mostly laps up the blood of big animals, like cows. It doesn't live in North America."

"Wow. I think you're spending too much time around Robbie," Suzie said. "His geekiness is rubbing off on you. You totally sounded just like him."

"What's wrong with that?" my mom said. "Robbie's a very smart little boy."

"He's a big science geek," Suzie said.

"He is not!" I said. "He's my best friend, so just shut up, Fathead!"

"All right, you two," my mom said. "Suzie, sit down and let Freddy do his report for you. He's nervous, so he needs to practice a bit in front of an audience."

"I don't want to do it for her."

"Well, I don't have time, anyway. I have to do my homework."

"You have five minutes," my mom said, leading Suzie over to a chair. "Just sit."

"Do I have to do it for her?"

"Yes, it's good practice. Now come on."

I recited my report.

When I was finished, my mom said, "See, Freddy, there's nothing to be nervous about. You just did great!"

"I don't get nervous in front of Suzie, Mom, but I know I'm just going to freeze up in front of the class."

"I was really nervous before my first oral report, too," Suzie said. "You know what Dad told me to do?"

"No, what?"

"He told me to just imagine everyone sitting there in their underwear. I did, and it was so funny, I totally forgot about being nervous."

"It really worked?"

"Yep."

Just then the phone rang, and my mom got up to answer it. "I'll be back in a minute."

"Your report is missing something, though," Suzie said.

"What?"

"Pictures. Kids like to see pictures."

"I could cut and paste these from the computer."

"They're not big enough."

"Well, with my arm like this, I can't draw any."

"I'll make some for you," Suzie said.

"Really? You'd do that for me?"

"I'll make you a deal. I will draw you pictures for your report, if you promise to carry your own backpack from now on instead of making me do it. You didn't break both your arms. Your left one still works, right?"

"But Mom and Dad . . ."

"Do we have a deal or not?"

"Deal," I said as we locked pinkies. Of course I had to use my left one. "You're the best sister in the whole world."

"I know."

CHAPTER 10

Teddy Bear Underwear

The next day at school when it was time to do our reports, Mrs. Wushy picked me to go first.

As I got up in front of the class, my stomach started doing flip-flops. I thought I was going to throw up right there, but then I remembered what Suzie told me and closed my eyes. I imagined everyone in his underwear. Chloe had on pink underwear with flowers and lace, but Max's were the best. He had on undies with little teddy bears. The biggest bully in all of first grade had teddy bear underwear!

"Are you OK, Freddy?" Mrs. Wushy whispered in my ear.

I opened my eyes and smiled a great big smile. "Yeah. I'm fine. Just great," I said. Then, with Robbie holding up my pictures, I recited my whole report perfectly.

When I finished, everybody clapped.

"Well, Freddy," said Mrs. Wushy, "you did a fabulous job, even with a broken arm. You should be proud of yourself."

I barely heard her. I was still thinking about Max in his teddy bear underwear.

DEAR READER,

I am both a teacher and a mom, so I really know how much kids hate homework! I know you love the weekends because then you don't have to do any homework. As a teacher, I have heard all the excuses for why kids don't have their homework: "I forgot it at home," "I left it in my mom's car," "I dropped it on the way to school," and of course, "My dog ate it." One time a little boy in my class told me his dog ate his homework. I didn't believe him until he showed me all the chewed-up pieces!

I hope you have as much fun reading *Homework Hassles* as I had writing it.

HAPPY READING!

Abby Klein

Freddy's Fun Pages

FREDDY'S
SHARK JOURNAL

A shark can never break a bone like I did.

Shark skeletons are not made of bone. They are made of cartilage.

Cartilage is very strong, but it can bend and is more flexible than solid bone.

You have cartilage in your nose and your ears.

Because a shark's skeleton is made of cartilage, a shark can turn and twist its body very quickly.

A VERY SILLY STORY
by Freddy Thresher

Help Freddy write a silly story by filling in the blanks
on the next two pages. The description under each
blank tells you what kind of word to use. Don't read
the story until you have filled in all the blanks!

HELPFUL HINTS:

A **verb** is an action word (such as run, jump, or hide).
An **adjective** describes a person, place, or thing
(such as smelly, loud, or blue).

I have a problem. A really, really, _____ problem.

an adjective

A_____ ate my homework! It all started because

a big animal

we had to write a _____-page report on_____.

a number   living things

Luckily,_____ has some in his_____. We took

a friend   a room in a house

the _____ out of their _____

the same living things   something you store things in

and observed them. They tried to_____ , but

a verb

we _____ them right away. Then, we ran
          a verb ending in -ed

downstairs to find a _____ and a _____
                    a vegetable   a type of junk food

to see which one they would rather _____.
                                        a verb

When we got back, _____'s pet _____,
                  the same friend   the same big animal

_____, was sitting on the _____
a really silly name   a piece of furniture

where we had left the _____. He
                        the same living things

looked very proud of himself. And then he burped!

"Oh no!" I wailed. "Your _____
                          the same big animal

ate our homework! What are we going to do?"

"Don't worry," said _____. "I also keep
                     the same friend

some _____ under my bed. We'll do a
       smelly living things

report on those instead. They're so _____
                                        an adjective

that _____ won't go near them!"
      the same really silly name

GO BATTY

Try making this stuffed bat to hang
upside down in your room.
—Freddy

1. Stuff a long, black sock with newspaper or stuffing.

2. Tie the open end into a knot.

3. Trace the wings and ears onto black construction paper or cardboard. Cut them out and glue them onto the stuffed sock as shown.

4. Trace the eyes onto white paper. Cut them out and glue them on.

5. Tie a string to the knotted end, and hang it upside down in your room or home.

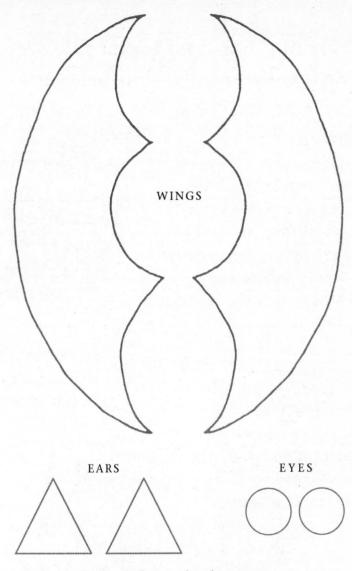

WINGS

EARS

EYES

You can also make these patterns
larger if you like.

Freddy has *another* problem— a really, really, big problem!

FREDDY THRESHER is in trouble with the class bully—again! Everyone knows that Max Sellars is the meanest kid in first grade. He'll push you, he'll punch you, and he'll even sit on your lunch! Can Freddy survive a competition with Max?

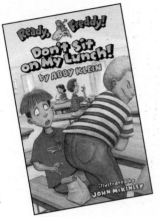

Find out in *Don't Sit on My Lunch!*

And don't miss Freddy's other adventures. . . .

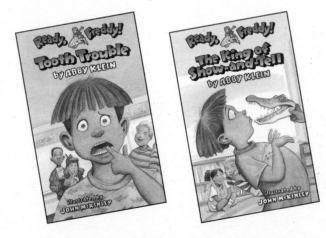